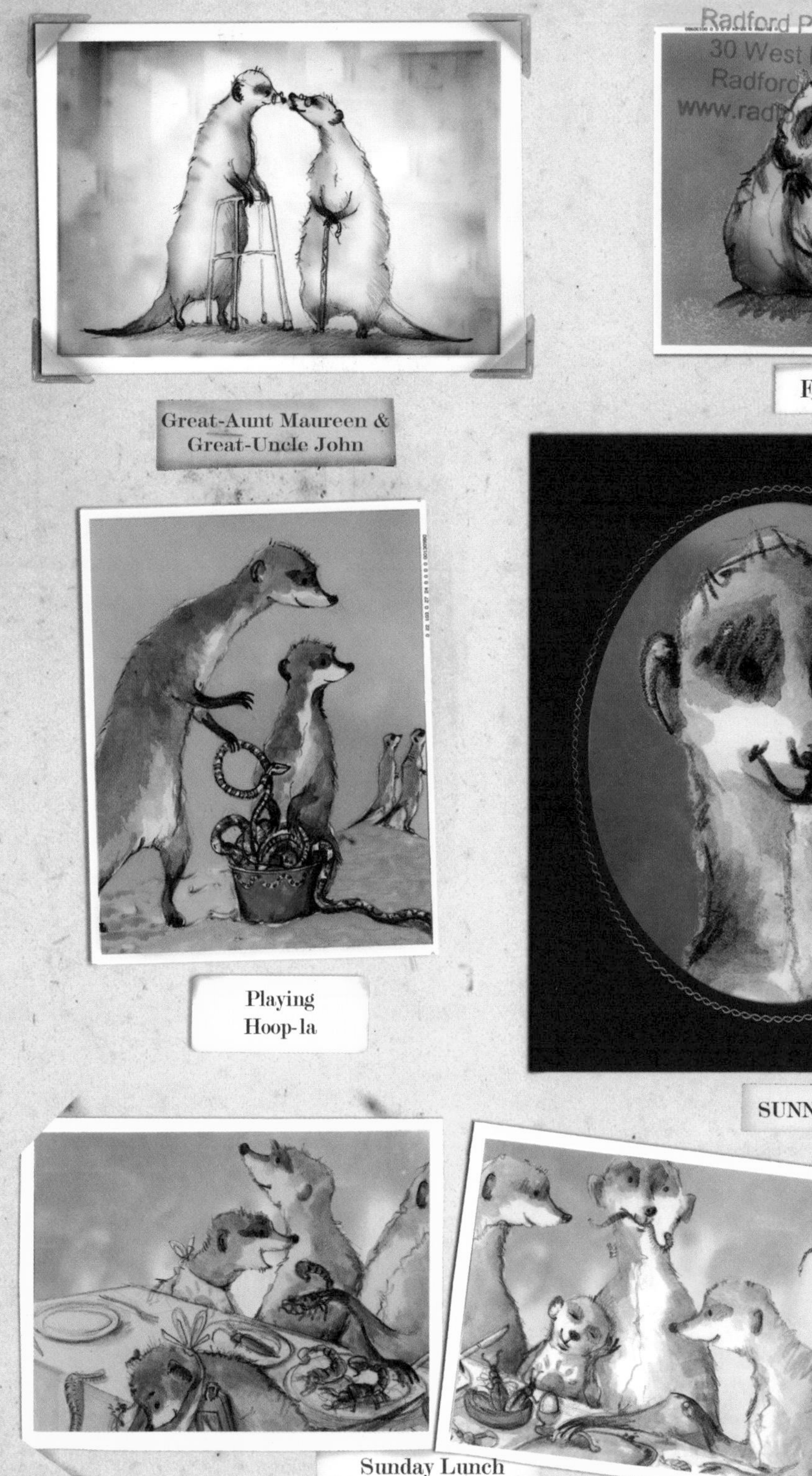

Great-Aunt Maureen &
Great-Uncle John

Playing
Hoop-la

Sunday Lunch
"The Mob Together"

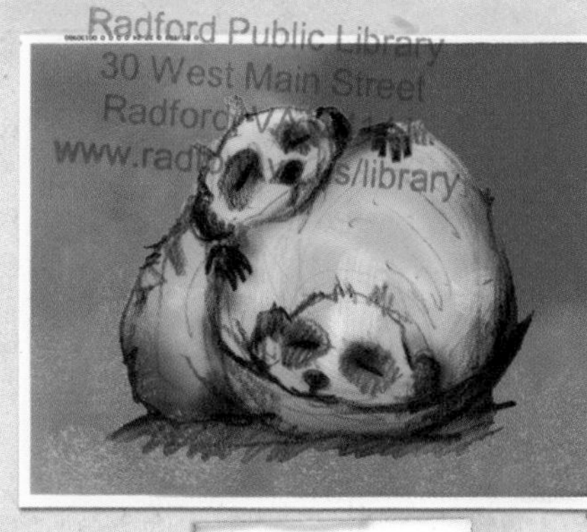

Florence's kids

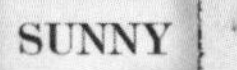

SUNNY

Clara

Sandcastle

Sandbath

This book is for my beautiful friend Zoe
(and her itchy feet).

SIMON & SCHUSTER BOOKS FOR YOUNG READERS
An imprint of Simon & Schuster Children's Publishing Division
1230 Avenue of the Americas, New York, New York 10020

Originally published in Great Britain in 2006 by Macmillan Children's Books, a division of Macmillan Publishers Limited
First U.S. edition 2007
Published by arrangement with Macmillan Children's Books

Manufactured in China
2 4 6 8 10 9 7 5 3 1
CIP data for this book is available from the Library of Congress.
ISBN-13: 978-1-4169-3473-8
ISBN-10: 1-4169-3473-1

Meerkat Mail

Emily Gravett

Simon & Schuster Books for Young Readers
New York London Toronto Sydney

Sunny lives in the Kalahari Desert.
It is VERY dry and VERY hot.
Sometimes Sunny thinks it is . . .

. . . TOO hot.

Sunny comes from a large family.
They work together,

play together,

eat together,

learn together . . .

and sleep together.

The Mongoose Family Tree
A Cousin In Every
Corner

In fact, they do everything together.
They are VERY close.

Sometimes Sunny thinks they are
TOO close.

Sometimes, Sunny wishes that he could live somewhere else.
So he packs his suitcase, and writes his family a note.

STAY SAFE
STAY TOGETHER

Dear Everyone

I'm off to find somewhere PERFECT to live.

(Don't worry Mom, I'll be staying with our Mongoose relatives, so will be quite safe)

Love from

X Sunny

~~toothbrush~~
~~Bucket~~
~~Toothpaste~~
~~Stamps~~

P.S. I promise to write

On Monday Sunny visits his Uncle Bob.

AFRICAN RED HORNBILL

warning mongoose of danger

Uncle Bob's family makes him very welcome.
But Sunny just doesn't fit in.

So on Tuesday Sunny goes to stay with his cousins Scratch and Mitch, and the rest of their family.

Sunny is getting itchy feet.
He decides it's time to move on!

On Wednesday he arrives at his cousin Edward's.

Sunny is not at all sure that eggs totally agree with him.

On Thursday he heads off to stay with his cousins Mildred and Frank.

Sunny hates getting wet, so he decides to leave.

By Friday evening Sunny has reached Madagascar.

Sunny is afraid of the dark. He can't think of anything worse . . .

Until on Saturday he arrives at Great-Aunt Flo's.

Sunny is beginning to worry that nowhere is right for him.

But then on Sunday Sunny arrives somewhere very dry and very hot, where *everyone* is very close.

And it is . . .

WELCOME HOME!

. . . perfect!

Mildred (or frank?)
Me with Scratch & M...
MOVING DA...
Ed's prize-winning
egg!
Photocard Number
260497
NAME OF HOLDER
Mr S. MEERKAT
Non-Transferable. See over for conditions.
This pass entitles the holder
to free travel anywhere.
Valid from now
until the foreseeable future.
Only to be used off-peak.
TRAVEL PHOTOCARD
SUNNY MEERKAT
THE MEERKAT MOB
SANDY BURROW
THE DUNES
KALAHARI DESERT
UNDER THE BIG BLUE SKY.
Big Red and Uncle Bob.
↑ME
Great-Aunt Flo ↑
Auntie B & Uncle Rob.
showing me how to dance!